Deeper In Life

Deeper In Life

James Watson

Copyright © 2021 by James Watson.

All rights reserved. No part of this book may be reproduced in any form or by any electronic or mechanical means, including information storage and retrieval systems, without permission in writing from the publisher, except by reviewers, who may quote brief passages in a review.

ISBN: 978-1-957054-36-0 (Paperback Edition)
ISBN: 978-1-957054-37-7 (Hardcover Edition)
ISBN: 978-1-957054-35-3 (E-book Edition)

Some characters and events in this book are fictitious. Any similarity to the real persons, living or dead, is coincidental and not intended by the author.

Book Ordering Information

Phone Number: 315 288-7939 ext. 1000 or 347-901-4920
Email: info@globalsummithouse.com
Global Summit House
www.globalsummithouse.com

Printed in the United States of America

TABLE OF CONTENTS

Dedication 1

2Pac & Biggie Smalls 3

9 minutes later 4

12 o'clock boyz 5

All dogs go to Heaven 6

All good things must come to an end 8

Amen 9

Angry black woman 10

Anything to protect her 11

Apple bottom jeans 12

Back rub 13

Baltimore crisis 14

Beauty and the Beast 15

Best friends now lovers 16

Black Fathers 17

Black History (What if) 19

Black Woman 20

Blood of Jesus 22

Bookworm 23

Breakfast in the morning 24

Brick wall 25

Bundle of Joy 26

C.u.s.s.i.n.g Can.U.Stop.Swearing.It's.Not like you.Girl 27

Calling on you 28

Capitol Punishment 29

Casino Love 30

Champion 31

Christmas Eve 32

Christopher Columbus 33

Closure 34

Clowns 35

Coming home for Christmas 36

Corona 37

Cream 38

Country Love 39

Criminal mind 40

Crossfire 41

Deebo dedicated to Tommy Tiny Lister 42

Dirty Laundry 43

Daddy's precious princess 44

Doctor Seuss	45
Donald Chump	46
Drama Queen	48
Drowning	50
Earthquake	51
Everything going to be alright just fight	52
Fairytale Nightmare 2	53
Firefighter	55
Gangstar R.I.P Guru	56
G.P.S-God's.Perfect.Son	57
Good woman	58
Halle Berry	59
Halloween	60
Handcuffs	61
He can't love you like I can	62
Hold me close	64
Housewife	65
How many more	67
How much can a man take	68
Hung	69
Hustler	70
I Am Erica	71

I found you 73

I thought it would be easy 74

I just want to end it 75

Ignorance 76

Illuminati 77

I'm a hero 78

Interstate 79

Iron Mike Tyson 80

Jacuzzi Love 81

Jagged Edge 82

Jobs 84

Just a little bit 85

Kamala Harris 86

Katrina 88

Knives 89

Last Days 90

Lead Me 91

Lebron James 92

Let your voice be heard 93

Life's a bitch 94

Light a candle 95

Like Mike dedicated to Michael Jordan 96

Lost	98
Lottery Ticket	99
Love and Hip Hop	100
Love in the club	102
Love in the studio	103
Loyal to the wrong one	104
Make it or Take it	105
Michael Jackson	106
Miracle Whip	107
Mistakes	108
Monster	109
Mr. Officer	110
My apology letter	111
Never Doubt Her	112
Never ever	114
No good in goodbye	115
No matter what you're going through	116
Not letting nothing get in my way	118
Nothing to Something	119
Oreo	121
Paul Mooney	122
Pinocchio	123

Piece of trash	124
Please don't shoot	125
Popping Pills	126
Precious Baby Girl	127
Rise	128
September 11 2021	129
Shaquille O'Neal	130
Single Mothers	131
Sleeping with the enemy	133
Sleepless in Seattle	134
So many	135
Sometimes	136
Taking credit for everything we do	137
Tell him	138
That's my son	140
The God I serve	141
The hill we climb dedicated to Amanda Gorman	143
The Ladawn Black Show	144
The only woman	145
The Plandemic	147
This isn't right	148
Trials and Tribulations	149

Trust in God 150

Unbelievable...151

Veteran Day 152

We shall overcome...153

Wendy Williams...155

What's Love..157

When we touch...158

Withdraw..159

Woman 160

You can still...161

You smell...162

You will not be satisfied...163

Your eyes 164

Zaytoven 165

Author Biography..167

Dedication

As always I would like to spread my love to my Lord and saviour Jesus Christ. Without him in my life to guide me. None of this would be possible. I dedicate this book to everyone who supported me throughout my career. This one is for you. I hope I made you proud.

2Pac & Biggie Smalls

These two brothers
Turn a whole coast against one another
It was a battle between east and west
To see who was the best
They were the best of friends
History was in the making
But at the end
Two lives were taken
These two brothers were branding
And expanding
The game of Hip Hop
They would still be here today
If it wasn't for a big misunderstanding
They died at the beginning of their prime
Could this murder be the most perfect crime
You heard the hurt in their
voice when they rhyme
They knew it was their time
At first it was all laughter and fun
But ended by the hands of a gun

By: James Watson

9 minutes later

The scars you put on my back
Reminds me why I'm black
You tried to cover up my death
When I simply told you that I was running out of breath
You didn't feel sorry for me
When you had your knee on my neck
You only felt sorry because I'm no longer here
And to cover everything up
They gave everyone a stimulus check
What you did was wrong
And in jail is where you belong
You had me pinned to the ground
While everyone else stood around
Which I thought was so unfair
I know you heard me gasping for air
If you didn't do what you did
I probably still be alive today
Coming home to my wife and kids
My life wasn't yours to take away
But since you thought that it was your authority
To do so
This is the price you have to pay

By:James Watson

12 o'clock boyz

Here comes the 12 o'clock boyz
And we making a whole lot of noise
Rolling through your hood
Always up to no good
Popping wheelies
And acting silly
You've never seen tricks like this before
As we terrorize the streets of Baltimore
We ride or die out here in these streets
So forget the cops
Everywhere we go
People give us their props
Some may say
We're obnoxious and rude
And that we ride with an attitude
But we're just having fun
We rather ride bikes
Then to sell drugs and bust guns

By:James Watson

All dogs go to Heaven

DMX you spit that rawness
And your lyrics were flawless
You gave the industry chills when you bark
Your bite was as vicious as a shark
You had the hood on lock
And everyone respected you
When you came on their block
You're one dog they couldn't keep on a leash
The world wasn't ready for your attack
You were so understanding
And always willing to give back
No one could walk in your shoes
Or tell stories the way you do
Only God knows what you've been through
So he thought it was best for you to come home
And bury your bone
That way you could join him
And be seated next to his throne
He seen how much you had to juggle
So he said
No more son do you have to struggle
Because I will give you peace
And you don't have to worry about nothing anymore

Your doves I will release
And your soul will be restored
Your death we mourn
And our hearts will forever be torn
But we must look at the bright side of it
An angel was just born

By:James Watson

All good things must come to an end

The game killed you
The fame killed you
Your name killed you
No one could do what you did on stage
Your temper was like an animal
Who has been locked up in a cage
No one could match your rage
They took you out at an early age
You were one of a kind
They feared your mind
They feared your grind
Art like this was hard to find
All good things must come to an end
Betrayed by your closest friends
A role model for thugs
The industry hated you
That's probably why they wanted to fill you up with slugs
Because you loved your music
Wasn't to concern about selling drugs
You spoke the truth
Every time you were in the booth
You did it for the incarcerated
And the youth

By:James Watson

Amen

Amen

I'm alive

Amen

I survive

Amen

I'm not who I used to be

Amen

I now have a testimony

Amen

I no longer have to fear

Amen

All my problems have disappear

Amen

I'm no longer poor

Amen

I don't have to worry about sleeping on the floor

Amen

I have finally found grace

Amen

I can now wipe the tears from my face

By:James Watson

Angry black woman

Why are you always mad
You can't keep a man
And that's sad
Everything about you is rude
And no one likes your stinking attitude
Why do you always like to fight
And no matter what I say
You're always right
You never like to admit
When you're wrong
So to keep you from fussing
I just play along
Because no matter what I say
You're still going to act the same way
You're never happy
And you're always feeling so crappy
Is your period coming on
Do you need a tampon
Because you're acting so mean right now

By:James Watson

Anything to protect her

A man will do anything for his wife
Even if that means giving up his own life
He will never make her wait
And will always make sure that she's straight
He will never ever play with heart
And never let anyone else
tear the two of them apart
He will never abuse her
Or use her
He will always be right by her side
He will always be there to provide
He will always treat her like a queen
He will never treat her like something
he can just get in between
He will never call her out her name
He will never play with her heart like it's a game
He will always treat her right
And he will never put his hands on her
Even if the two of them get into a fight

By:James Watson

Apple bottom jeans

Girl your butt looks mean
In them apple bottom jeans
You love how they fit
Showing off your rear end
Because they might split
If you bend
Guys get so pump
When they see your rump
Because them apple bottom jeans
Make you look so plump
I just want to slap you on the ass
Every time I see you walk pass
I know everyday you have to fight
Just to put them on
Because they fit you so tight
But they feel just right

By:James Watson

Back rub

I'm going to give your body a good scrub
While we make love right here in this tub
Take my sponge out
And give you a back rub
Cover you in some suds
Surround you with rose buds
Touching you in places that's
hard for you to reach
You want to get wet
This is the closest thing to a beach
Rubbing on your peach
While I'm sucking on your body like a leach
You can give me sucky sucky
While you're squeezing on my rubber ducky
And if you're lucky
I might rub you down with some oil
Because you deserve to be spoiled

By:James Watson

Baltimore crisis

Baltimore have some real issue
And it all starts with the officials
Stop saying what you're going to do
And do something about it
Because we're sick and tired
Of seeing people dying over some bullshit
They don't care how the city looks
Because most of them are a bunch of crooks
And shouldn't be left off the hook
They claim they're doing everything by the book
They need to do something about the crime
And stop wasting our time
They need to stop acting like some sissy
And be more tough
Because enough is enough
We can't hope for the best
Until we put this thing to rest

By:James Watson

Beauty and the Beast

Baby does beauty really matter
When you look in the mirror
And all it does is shatter
You say that you're ugly
And all it does is make you look fatter
Baby where you self esteem
Sometimes the things in the mirror
Isn't always what it seems to be
You have to love yourself regardless
Of what you see
The mirror doesn't lie or hide
Who you are on the outside
No matter what anyone says
You're beautiful in so many ways
If your mirror didn't crack
Then you're okay
Take a step back
And don't let what anyone has to say
Ruin your day
Because beauty will never fade away

By:James Watson

Best friends now lovers

No one knows you
Better than I do
How did it come to this
Am I guilty for giving you a kiss
Did we cross the line
Now I can't get you out of my mind
Lets keep this on the down low
Because I don't want no one else to know
I don't want this to ruin a good friendship
We both got caught slipping
We broke a friendship rule
But I'm not tripping
Maybe I went too far
When I stuck my hand in the cookie jar
I should have asked first
Before I done that
I wish I can take it back
But it's too late
We might as well go on a date

By:James Watson

Black Fathers

You call us deadbeats
Who always like to cheat
On our women
You call us thugs
Who always like to sell drugs
You call us uneducated
You say we're filled with hatred
You say that we will never succeed
When it comes to a white man
You say all we like to do is drink and smoke weed
And that's why we can't do what they can do
Because we're obsessed with greed
You say most of us will be dead
Or in jail
You say most of us will not get ahead
That we will fail
We get treated so unfair
Because of the color of our skin
And the nappiness of our hair
We're not always abandoning our kids
We're not always doing bids
We just want the same respect
You show them

Because we're not always the problem
All of the time
Because to be a black father
In this world is a crime

By:James Watson

Black History (What if)

What if Harriet Tubman never ran
What if she never had a plan
To free her people from the white man
What if Martin Luther King never had a dream
What if Jackie Robinson never
made the Brooklyn Dodgers team
What if Malcolm X never been shot
What if Rosa Parks never had a boycott
What if Muhammad Ali never fought
What if Frederick Douglass never had a thought
What if Maya Angelou never wrote
What if Marcus Garvey never made his quote
What if Loretta Mary Aiken never told a joke
What if Angela Davis never spoke
What if they never pave the way
For us to be here today
What would life be like
What if

By: James Watson

Black Woman

Black woman
You're a Nubian Queen
Black woman
You're the most influential person
the world has ever seen
Black woman
Your skin is beautiful and bold
Black woman
You're worth more than any money or gold
Black woman
Your beauty is ageless
Black woman
You have so much finesse
Black woman
I love the nappiness of your hair
Black woman
When it comes to your heart no one can compare
Black woman
You're such a work of art
Black woman
You're so intelligent and smart
Black woman
I love your full lips
Black woman

I love your curvy hips
Black woman
You don't take mess from no one
Black woman
When you say you're done
You're done
Black woman
I love how hood you can be
Black woman
No matter what they say about you
I know you'll be there for me

By:James Watson

Blood of Jesus

If it wasn't for the blood you shed
Would I have found my glory
The crown on your head
Tells another story
Your blood will never lose its power
It will always be sweet
And never be sour
As I kneel down to your feet
Your blood is pure
Your blood is the cure
Your blood washes all my sins away
Your blood is the reason why I'm here today
Your blood is the reason why I survive
Your blood is the reason why I'm alive
Your blood runs through my veins
Your blood relieves me from my pain
Your blood is the reason why I never like to complain
Your blood is the reason why I have so much to gain

By:James Watson

Bookworm

They say don't judge a book by its cover
Because in this story
I'm looking for the perfect lover
This book isn't for all ages
So make sure you read it
Before you flip through the pages
Fiction or non fiction
Does this book fits your description
Keep the lights on
Because it can hurt your eyes
If you try to read in the dark
And if you want to pick up where we left off
Don't forget your bookmark
This book is so good
You'll want to read it from the begining
To the end
This book is so good
You'll want to tell a friend
I'm such a bookworm
And I will read it in all languages
Because I understand all terms

By:James Watson

Breakfast in the morning

Sex is like breakfast in the morning
It feels good to wake up to a meal
At the break of dawn
I feel great
After a good stretch and yawn
I can smell your coffee brewing straight from the pot
And your food got steam coming from it
Which means it's nice and hot
Just like some flatjacks
I want to turn you over to your back
And pull my syrup all over it
It's hot and sticky like some grits
As I kneel down
And open up your legs
Pull out my fork
And eat your scramble eggs
I'm not the one who likes to eat pork
But your bacon taste so good
It must be apple wood
Spread my jelly
All over your toasted bread
I just love a good breakfast in bed

By: James Watson

Brick wall

Girl it's like talking to a brick wall
I don't think you hear me at all
We're not going anywhere with this conversation
So why should I waste my time even talking to you
Because you're going to do
What you want to do anyway
No matter what I say
Because talking to you is pointless
And I don't need the stress
How can you look me in the face
And not say one word
When I know you heard
Me in the first place
You can't keep walking around
And not make one sound
Because sooner or later
I'm going to knock your brick wall down

By:James Watson

Bundle of Joy

You're my baby boy
And mommy's bundle of joy
I hope when you grow up
You find someone like your mama
Who doesn't cause you trauma
Or bring you any kind of drama
I expect you to hold the family down
When your fathers not around
I will teach you everything you need to know
I will nourish you
And give you everything you need to help you grow
Into the man you need to be
Love your wife
The same way you would have loved me
Never put your hands on her
Protect her
And never neglect her
You're my little King
I promise to give you everything
I promise to always be the wind beneath your wings

By:James Watson

C.u.s.s.i.n.g Can.U.Stop.Swearing.
It's.Not like you.Girl

Why do you like to use so much profanity
Then you blame it on your insanity
When I get you mad
You can't say a entire sentence without cussing
Girl swearing to God is bad
So you need to say something
else when you're fussing
Your mouth is so file
But you've been using profanity for a while
So I'm not expecting you to change now
I just don't like how this situation is going down
I think it's unlady like
That you have to express yourself this way
You said boy take a hike
You think I give a damn what
you or anyone else have to say
You can't tell me what to say when I'm mad
If you don't like what I say out my mouth
Oh well too bad
I know you say things you don't mean
When you're upset
Your mouth is so flithy and needs to be clean
Before you say something that you might regret

By:James Watson

Calling on you

Lord I'm calling on you

Save my soul

Rearrange my life

And make me whole

I can't do it alone

So if you hear your phone ringing

Please answer your phone

I know you're busy

And you have a lot on your plate

I'll just wait patiently for you at the pearly gates

I have some problems I need you to take care of

And the only place I could look was above

Lord I don't mean to bug you

But there's nothing in this world

I would want more than to hug you

I'll just wait my turn in line

Because I know you have a lot
of problems to deal with

Other than mines

By:James Watson

Capitol Punishment

There's no excuse for what they did
If that was a black man
They would have been put a bullet in our head
What they did wasn't right
They just mad because their president loss a fair fight
Who let them across
Why didn't they fight back
Why didn't they use some kind of kombat
I bet you if they were black
They would have use some kind of attack
We would have been maced in our face
What they did was a disgrace
To the entire human race
Trump supporter all over the place
They acted like animals
Who just been released from a cage
They barged their way in with rage
They shouldn't have made it pass the first stage
Why didn't they use some kind of force
Because they were white of course
This was uncalled for
And shouldn't have happened this way
They need to be arrested and locked away
Someone has to pay
For what went down today

By:James Watson

Casino Love

I'm going to put my quarter
In her slot
I'm will not stop until I give her a son or daughter
I will not stop until I hit the jackpot
We're playing strip poker
I must play my cards right
So I hit her with a joker
And she was done for the rest of the night
I told her to grab my dice
And give them a blow
It's for good luck
Now give them a real good throw
I'm placing my bet
I'm laying it all on the line
I will not forfeit
Until she's all mine
Sometimes you have to trust your gut
Because if I hit it big
I'm giving her half of my cut
They call this sin city
And I will not stop until I win baby

By:James Watson

Champion

We've made it this far
There's no stopping us now
Lets keep on going
Until we reach for the stars
Because nothing going to keep us down
Our mission isn't done
Until we're crowned number one
Many tried to beat us
But they could never defeat us
There's a new champion in town
There's a new champion about to be crown
Our main goal
Is to become the best
And we will not rest
Until we've accomplish our quest
We're making a name for ourselves
To prove to the world
That we're better than everyone else
We crushing anyone that comes in our way
We're winning against anyone that we play

By:James Watson

Christmas Eve

I never knew why it was so hard
to sleep on Christmas Eve

All I keep thinking about is all the
wonderful gifts I'm going to receive

As a little boy

The day before Christmas always bring me so much joy

Because all I can think about is seeing a toy

Leaving cookies on the table

That Mom just bake

Hoping to see them gone

When I awake

Listening to Christmas songs

All night long

Is it morning time yet

I can't wait to see what I'm going to get

But I will not be able to see my surprise

Until I lay down to sleep

And close my eyes

By:James Watson

Christopher Columbus

This country was stolen by a white European
The true native of this land
Was discovered by a Native American
So why should they die
Just to get a piece of the American pie
This country was built on lies
He's nothing but a thief
And killed anyone
Who didn't believe in his belief
The women were rape
And he murdered anyone
Who tried to escape
The Indians were already here on these grounds
Before he came around
So how he going to say
That this was the country that he found
His holiday should be taken away
Because this lie has left us in disarray

By:James Watson

Closure

I can't do this anymore
It hurts too much
I need some closure
Maybe one day I'll keep in touch
I don't know when
But until then
This is how it's going to be
I think this is the best thing for you and me
It hurts to walk away
But it will hurt even more if I stay
You'll get over me one day
We need to stop pretending
Like this story is going to end with a happy ending
When we know it's not
We both been throught a lot
And we need time to heal from this
And that's the reason why I'm ending this relationship
So neither one of us have to deal with this

By:James Watson

Clowns

I didn't know the circus was in town
Because all I see now
Is a bunch of clowns
You want to be down
So bad
But instead of making me laugh
You make me frown
Always joking around
I wish I could wipe that smile
Off your face
Some of you are so file
And need to be put in your place
I never seen so many cornballs
You're not funny at all
Most of you know
How to put on a good show
Cosigning to everything that I say
Who does that anyway
You clowns do
But this time the joke is on you
So ha ha to you too

By:James Watson

Coming home for Christmas

I can't wait until you come home
I know you're over seas
And you're feeling all alone
I can't wait to see your face
I can't wait until you wrap me in your arms
And I can feel your warm embrace
I can't wait to lay up with you at the firepalce
I can't wait to unwrap gifts with you all night long
While we're singing and listening to Christmas songs
I hope you got all the letters
That I sent you
But to have you next to me is so much better
I wonder where all those days went to
I didn't think I would ever see you again
I worried about you a lot
But when you should up at my place
A whole lot of joy from within
Was happy that I got
A chance to see your face

By:James Watson

Corona

You tried to beat us
But we will not let you defeat us
You had us walking around in fear
But we will overcome you
Even if it takes us all year
You may have changed how we live today
You may have taken many lives away
Even though we're six feet apart
You can never take away the
love we have in our hearts
You made it hard for us to cope
You tried to take away our hope
You tried to seperate us away from our love one
But we refused to let go of this rope
One thing about us
We're strong
And when you thought you had us
You can only keep us down but for so long
One day we will find a vaccine
I miss those days
When we could stand next to one another
Because now we're in quarantine
We forgot how it feels to be together

By:James Watson

Cream

I love cream in my coffee
I love to lick the cream in between a cookie
I especially love to see the cream
coming from your nookie
You make me scream
For your ice cream
As it drips from my lips
I love to drink your cream soda
As I kneel down and take a sip
So creamy and rich
My tongue in between your legs
I call this a ice cream sandwich
I love cream cheese
As I spread some on your bagel
Once I taste your boston cream pie
You'll be begging for me to let go
I want to taste your Krispy Kreme doughnut
As you fill my gut
With your creamy filling

By:James Watson

Country Love

Things are a little different down south
I can tell that you're not from around here
By the words that's coming out from your mouth
Grits and eggs
Toast and strawberry jelly
You love to cook a good meal
You make sure I leave with a filled belly
No one can cook like you can
It's nice and warm down here
Cooking fried chicken in a cast iron pan
Come where the weather is great
Honey butter biscuits
And country chicken fried steak
Your lemonade and sweet tea so sweet
I can't wait to taste your sweet potato pie
Make me want to suck on some pig feet
Onions and liver
Smoothed in gravy
I love to go fishing by the river
My stomach is full
Now a brother lazy
Yeah I talk a little funny
If you're tired of the cold weather
Come down here where it's nice and sunny

By:James Watson

Criminal mind

A killer leaves no evidence behind
When he attacks
Making it hard for anyone to find
He tracks
He thrist for more
Leaving behind blood and gore
It gives him the chills
Every time he kills
And he gets a thrill
Seeing someone's blood spill
He has no feelings in his heart
And killing is his main art
Most killers are very smart
And it's something about them
That separates them apart
From everyone else
He doesn't care about you
Or himself
He has no remorse
For what he does

By:James Watson

Crossfire

Some lines you don't cross
Someone should have told you
That you're messing with a boss
Like trash
You're about to get toss
Because messing with me
You're about to receive your first loss
You've crossed the wrong path
Now you're about to feel my wrath
You better hope someone come and save you
On your behalf
Because this could end in a bloodbath
You're messing with the wrong one
Now look what you did
You've gone
And made someone like me mad
The worst thing you could have ever done
I'm really about to bring the bitch out of me
Someone I know you don't want to see

By:James Watson

Deebo dedicated to Tommy Tiny Lister

Here comes a six foot dude on a bike
Beating these dudes down like Iron Mike
Tuck in your chain
Here come this big dude again
Mean mugging
This dude Deebo be bugging
You know when he comes around
You better not make one sound
Or you will catch a beatdown
He doesn't care what you're talking about
Give it up quick
Or get knocked the fuck out
A bully no doubt
When you hear that music
And see that plague shirt
You know somebody about to get hurt
Deebo don't play
Especially on Friday
So empty your pockets
Or you will pay

By:James Watson

Dirty Laundry

I guess I have to come clean
Before I throw these clothes in the wash machine
I've done a lot of dirt
I caused you a lot of hurt
Like a wash cycle
What goes around comes around
I'm in hot water now
I need something strong to take away these stains
So I tried to use some gain
But that still wasn't enough to wash away the pain
Sorry if I made you cry
Now it's time for me to hang
my clothes out to dry
I had to seperate the color from the white
If I'm ever going to get this right

By:James Watson

Daddy's precious princess

You're Daddy little princess
What the two of you have is priceless
He will always be there to alarm you
From men that will try to harm you
He's your sword and shield
And you're his force field
He will lay down his life for you
Because he knows you'll do the same too
Watch out for these so call men
They like to play a lot of games
Never let him disrespect you
Or call you out of your name
And if he can't talk to you without using his hands
He isn't no man
A real man will understand
And give you all that he can

By:James Watson

Doctor Seuss

Let me play with your cat in the hat
While I give you a pity pat
Right on your booty
Because it's so phat
Call me Sam I am
Because I want to eat your green eggs and ham
There's a wocket in my pocket
And I can't wait to put it in your socket
Did I ever tell you how lucky you are
To be making love to a porn star
She told me to blow out her
candles and make a wish
I told her I want
One fish
Two fish
Red fish
Blue fish
Oh the places you'll go
Once you go down below
She told me to hop on pop
I said I will
And once I do
I'm not going to stop
Until I blow your top

By: James Watson

Donald Chump

You're the worst president we've ever had
Always talking about Obama
But he wasn't this bad
You don't care what you say
And because of that
America has to pay
I can't believe they voted you in
With your toupee and bleached skin
I hope when election day comes you don't win
America biggest fear
Is having you in office for four more years
You're the most ignorant
Most arrogant
Disrespectful person this country has ever seen
You better be lucky someone doesn't
run up in the White House
And kidnap you and your spouse
For running your mouth
No one cares about what you're tweeting
Or who you're meeting and greeting
You're always sweeping things under the rug
But got the nerve to call us thugs
When you're the main one
looking like you're on drugs

How are you going to lie to our face
And say that it's not about race
This use to be the greatest country in the land
Until they put the power into your hand
We the people have the power and showed that
Our ancestors are coming back to take what's ours
The money in your pocket belongs to us
Since our ancestors picked it
Now we want it back

By:James Watson

Drama Queen

You're such a drama queen
Always making a scene
Why are you so dramatic
Always causing so much static
You're always getting caught up
In a whole lot of mess
You should win an award
For best supporting actress
Sometimes you take things to over board
You be doing to much
I only gave you a little touch
And there you go
Falling all over the place
I thought that you were playing
But you had the serious look on your face
You can't be serious right now
I didn't even touch you
For you to be falling to the ground
You're always exaggerating
Over the littlest things
One thing I can say about you

Is that you sure know

How to play a role

And you know how to give your
audience a good show

By:James Watson

Drowning

I feel myself going down
Someone throw me a life jacket before I drown
No time to think
The more I keep it on my mind
The more I started to sink
Gasping for air
Holding on by the string of my hair
No time to hesitate
Someone come and rescue me
Before it's too late
Where's a lifeguard when you need one
I better get some help soon
Or I'm done
Trying to keep my head
Above sea level
If nothing else could go wrong
It just did
Lord I don't have long
Please tell me someone is on their way
I'm not dying
At least not today

By: James Watson

Earthquake

The bedroom is shaking
Everything around us is breaking
Can you feel my aftershock
The neighbors can feel us down the block
Ten point zero on the rector scale
We're are you going to hide
The bed is rocking from side to side
Put on your seat belt
Because you're about to go for a bumpy ride
Heaven and earth has collide
The walls are starting to crack
Nothing can prepare me for your impact
Could this be the end of civilization
Or is this the start of a abomination
No matter how you look at it
This could be the end of all of God's creation

By:James Watson

Everything going to be alright just fight

When you feel like the world is on your shoulders
And all your problems seem as heavy as a boulder
Everything going to be alright just fight
When you feel like you're having a bad day
And things aren't going your way
Everything going to be alright just fight
When it feels like you can't go on
And all your hope is gone
Everything going to be alright just fight
When life seems to beat you down
And you need someone to lift you off the ground
Everything going to be alright just fight

By:James Watson

Fairytale Nightmare 2

Humpty Dumpty sat on the wall
Humpty Dumpty had a great fall
The world just look at him as a crackhead
Instead of trying to go and get him some help
He just rather get high instead
All of Humpty friends
Couldn't put him back together again
He had a friend named Goldie locks
Who got high off of crack rock
She couldn't bear the fact
That she gets high off of crack
Her mind was as slow as a tortoises
Trying to kick her habit
She couldn't stay still like a rabbit
Her heart was starting to race
Life was too much for her to face
So she called her girlfriend
Little Miss Muffet
And the both of them sat on a tuffet
And started to puff it
Then came along this drug dealer
They called the big bad wolf
Who just wanted to blow their house down

Every time he came around
He couldn't stand these pigs they called cops
That was always trying to put a stop
On everything he did
This story wasn't meant for kids
And this is a story no one wants to tell
About a couple of friends who life was hell
I hope they get the help that they need
Before any one of them end up in jail

By:James Watson

Firefighter

He thought he could burn you down

But then someone like me
came and turn you around

You're exhausted from the heat

How could he tell you he love you

If he's going to cheat

He gave you no warning

He let you walk right into a burning building

And didn't have the guts to try
and save you or your children

You could have died from the smoke

But thanks to God

All it did was make you choke

Let me put out his flames

Because I know you're tired of him playing games

No need to call 9-1-1

Because when you're done

You're done

No more will he cause you any kind of harm

Because if he does

Just ring the alarm

And I'll be right there

By:James Watson

Gangstar R.I.P Guru

Let me take a minute in the booth
To kick a moment of truth
I'm so ill
Plus I got the skillz
To pay the bills
My mass appeal
Is too real
For these streets
I got the rhythms
And my man Premier got the beats
I don't play hard
But when I come around
Suckas need bodyguards
My royalty
Isn't hard to earn
And loyalty
Is hard to learn
You know my steez
I bring Mc's to their knees
Battling these cats in the industry is a breeze
Any M.C run up on me better freeze
Before I cock back and squeeze
This desert eeze

By:James Watson

G.P.S - God's. Perfect. Son

Follow him
And he will lead you in the right direction
We were made in the image of his reflection
Follow him
And you will never be lost
Because he took all of our sins to the cross
When you find yourself in a unfamiliar place
Turn to his grace
He will never send you the wrong way
All you have to do is listen to what he has to say
And you will be okay
When you find yourself going
down the wrong route
He will find you a way out
You'll never be lost with him by your side
Trust in him and he'll be your guide

By:James Watson

Good woman

I got me a good woman at home
Who loves me a lot
Who can clean and cook
I got me a good woman
Who doesn't care how much money I got
And who doesn't care how I look
I got a good woman
Who tells me everything going to be alright
When we get into a fight
I got me a good woman
Who rubs my back at night
I got me a good woman
Who doesn't put me down
And when I fall she'll lift me up from the ground
I got a good woman
Who shows me loyalty
And who gives me royalty
I got a good woman
Who gives me her everything
And who treats me like a King

By:James Watson

Halle Berry

Halle Berry you got some big monster's ball
Looking down on people
Who doesn't have it all
Like you do
You can't treat people like anything
And don't think it's not going to happen to you
Like a boomerang
What goes around comes around
You think you're the baddest
women on this earth
Until you've been through the storm
Then you will see the bulworth
You've been talking all along
How you treat people is wrong
You better be glad no one doesn't
kidnap your ass one day
For treating people this way
You probably get away with this in Hollywood
But you will never get away
with this in the hood

By:James Watson

Halloween

Goblins and goons
Wolves hollowing at a full moon
Zombies and mummies
Bobbing for apples
Eating worms made from gummies
Curving pumpkins
And watching the little munchkins
Go trick or treating
Candy corn
And creepy masks being worn
Spooky ghost tales
And costumes for sale
Black cats
And witches hats
Watching horror movies all night long
Listening to the monster bash song
Trick or treat
Smell my feet
Give me something good to eat

By:James Watson

Handcuffs

You say these handcuffs are too tight
You've been a bad girl
Now it's time for me to read you your rights
As I slap
These handcuffs on your wrist
You're trap
No matter how hard you tried to resist
Your arrest
Once these handcuffs are on you
I not letting you go
Until you're in jail
And I'm not letting you out
Until you can find someone to pay your bail
If you do the crime
You have to do the time

By:James Watson

He can't love you like I can

You feel all alone
You're living in a broken home
I can hear you crying on the other side of the phone
I asked you what's wrong
You said you can't do this anymore
I can't see how you stayed with him this long
You said that this relationship
was making your heart sore
I don't mean to cry in your ears
Go ahead and cry baby
I wish I was there to wipe away your tears
At least you gave it a try baby
I know you're hurting
But if it ain't working
It's not working
You can walk away anytime you feel like it
You crazy
Because I would have been
walked away from his bullshit
I would have been packed my things and split
How many times do you have to be hit
For you to realize he ain't shit
You know I'm right
Who do you call

Every time the to of you get into a fight
Who do you call
Every time he sends you to bed crying every night
He ain't no man
If he puts his hands on you
He can't love you like I can
So what are you going to do
Stay
Or walk away

By:James Watson

Hold me close

Lord hold me close to your heart
The devil is trying to tear us apart
Keep me in your arms
Keep me away from harm
Even when I feel myself slipping away
Even when I feel myself falling astray
You extended your arms out
And gave me a place to stay

By:James Watson

Housewife

I thought I could change your life
I thought I could turn a hoe into a housewife
You will not cook
You will not clean
You don't care how you look
And your attitude is mean
I thought I could take a girl
Like you out of the hood
Treat you good
And that would be it
Man was I wrong
I should have left you right where you belong
You don't do nothing anyway
But give me a headache all day
Get up off your lazy ass and get a job
But yet you want to lay around the house
And live like a slob
You will not change the kids pamper
You will not wash the clothes in the hamper
All you do is eat up all the food
And you wonder why when I come home
I'm in a bad mood
Because of things like this

You know I'm out here working hard
You will not even give me a hug or kiss
But that's what I get
For trying to turn a hoe into a housewife
Because all you did was ruining my life

By:James Watson

How many more

How many more have to go down
How many more have to hit the ground
How many more must die
How many more must cry
How many more must mourn
How many more will be left torn
How many more times are they
going to use the same excuse
How many more times are we
going to take this abuse
How many more times do our
mothers have to bury their love one
How many more times are they going
to keep shooting our daughter and son
How many more times are they
going to keep killing our black men
How many more times are they going to
keep throwing our black men in the pin
How many more times are we going to protest
How many more times are they going to
keep letting these cops get away with murder
Before they make a arrest
How many more

By:James Watson

How much can a man take

How much
Can one man take
Before he starts to break
How long
Is he going to hold on
After he finds out
That you been treating him so wrong
He will get tired eventually
I know you didn't mean to hurt him intentionally
But when he's fed up
He's fed up
And there's no telling what he'll do
Once he erupt
The best thing to do in this situation
Is to give him some space
Don't be all up in his face
Nagging
And getting on his nerve
Or you might get something
That you may not deserve

By:James Watson

Hung

She say I'm hung
That I got her sprung
If you're not packing
Then you're lacking
It looks like I'm walking with a third leg
She wants it bad
I told her that you don't have to beg
Either way you're going to get this nutmeg
She said that I'm hung like a horse
And can I take her for a ride around the course
She doesn't like it small
Because if it can't touch her wall
She doesn't want it at all
She wants to feel it in her gut
Until it have her walking funny with a strut
If you're not 12 inches or more
Don't you think that you're going to score

By:James Watson

Hustler

I love a woman who stays on her grind
I love a woman with money on her mind
I love a woman who's a boss
I love a woman who can floss
I love a woman who puts business before pleasure
I love a woman who goes way beyond her measures
I love a woman with skills
I love a woman who pays her own bills
I love a woman who can get the job done
I love a woman who doesn't answer to no one
I love a woman who loves to ball
I love a woman who makes her own call

By:James Watson

I Am Erica

I Am Erica
And this is just another day in America
I woke up to the crack of dawning
But this isn't one of my typical morning
Killing all across the state
We're supposed to be Untied
How much are we going to tolerate
This country is filled with so much hate
Racism still exist
And they still putting handcuffs
on our black men wrist
They say we're the home of the brave
But we're the home of the slaves
They want us to pledge allegiance to the flag
But yet our black men keep ending up in a body bag
This country is a joke
That's why I must stay woke
Because if I'm not
This country will take me for everything that I have
And leave me broke
This country was built on immigrants
Now we don't want them in our country

This isn't the American way
This country is about freedom
And those who gave their lives up
Each and everyday

By:James Watson

I found you

I thank God I found you
And now that you're here
I always want to be around you
Because my love for you isn't going anywhere
God put us together for a reason
You're reason why I'm alive and breathing
I will not stop until you're mine
You're the reason why the sun shines
I don't mind crossing that line
Between love and hate
I'll do anything for my soulmate
I know we're not getting any younger
But it's never too late
This is the commitment I'm willing to make
This is the sacrifice I'm willing to take
I can't wait until the day
I give myself away
To you
When I say
I do

By:James Watson

I thought it would be easy

I thought it would be easy
If I let you know
I thought it would be easy
If I let you go
I thought it would be easy
If I tell this to your face
I thought it would be easy
If I show up at your place
I thought it would be easy
If I gave you a call
I thought it would be easy
If I didn't tell you at all
I thought it would be easy
If we just sit down and talk
I thought it would be easy
If we just go for a walk
I thought it would be easy
If I get this off my chest
I thought it would be easy
If I lay this situation to rest

By:James Watson

I just want to end it

I just want to end it
Take my fragile heart
And just bend it
Because my soul is torn apart
Life isn't fair
And I just want to pull out my hair
Because I'm going insane
I can't deal with the pain
Trying to escape the rain
So many things I can't explain
I have nothing left to gain
I should just end it
Right here
Right now
Because no one cares
If I'm no longer around
I rather be buried six feet into the ground
My life is a mess
And I feel worthless

By:James Watson

Ignorance

There's low tolerance
For showing ignorance
People aren't born with racism in their heart
It's taught
And this is the main thing that
tearing us as a people apart
There's no excuse for the way we act
Everyone has their opinion on racism
But don't have the facts
Knowledge we lack
And this is the main thing that's holding us back
The world is divided
And we as people are misguided
The color of our skin
Shouldn't define us from within
Racism is a big issue that no one wants to talk about
Don't keep it in
Let it out
Because if we don't say something now
There's no telling how long this
thing is going to stick around
We're all equal
So let's show some love people

By: James Watson

Illuminati

People selling their soul for fame
People selling their soul just for a name
People getting killed
And it's not a game
If you're not like them
Then you're a problem
They have a way of disguising themselves
From everyone else
They will kill
You over a dollar bill
They will sacrifice what they love
Just to get ahead
And they will not stop
Until some blood has been shed
Just think about all the one's who has reach the top
And now they're dead
It's a shame
But it's all apart of fame

By:James Watson

I'm a hero

Because I risk my life everyday
To make sure that you're okay
I'm a hero
Because I do whatever I can
To give you a helping hand
I'm a hero
Because whenever you need me I'm always there
To show you my love support and care
I'm a hero
Because there's nothing I wouldn't do
To show you how much I care for you
I'm a hero
Because I want to help you succeed
And to be there to help you when you're in need
I'm a hero
Because I give it my all
To make sure that you don't fall
And that what makes me a hero

By:James Watson

Interstate

I caught a flat tire
Right on the interstate
There was a nail in my tire
And it's slowly starting to inflate
To make matters worse
I needed a hot wire
My engine was starting to catch on fire
This isn't going good right now
So I put some water in it
Just to cool it down
I'm having a bad day
So I called triple A
They said that they were on their way
Don't you go anywhere
We will be right there
I told them that I wasn't going anywhere
That I would be right here
Thank God for them
Because this is one problem
I couldn't fix
They told me they would be there
Somewhere around six

By:James Watson

Iron Mike Tyson

Pound for pound
He was the best fighter around
Furious and quick
Smooth and slick
His punches was as hard as a brick
In his prime
He was the best in his time
Coming from a background
Where he committed a lot of crime
He received the name Iron Mike Tyson
Because was as strong as a bison
Other fighters feared him
Every time he stepped in the ring
Because they knew the excitement he would bring
He was small
But a true wrecking ball
And when he hit you
It felt like you ran into a brick wall

By:James Watson

Jacuzzi Love

I know how to get you wet
It's so hot in here
We're starting to break a sweat
Have a seat
Sit down and feel this heat
The water is so hot
But it's touching all the right spot
I been in here
All day
And all night
And the way
You got me feeling
Is so right

By:James Watson

Jagged Edge

He said he promise to be a better man
But he can't love U like I can
Every since he gave you the keys to the range
His whole attitude change
I will never do you like that
Now he's trying to find the word's to say
To get you back
But the more he tried to redeemed himself
The more it made you want to walk away
He said that you were a ten
But to me you're an eleven
And all he did was put you through hell
He can't see that you walked outta heaven
Either he's the dumbest man on earth
Or I gotta be the smartest man
To see what you're really worth
He got the nerve to get on one knee
And tell you
Let's get married
You're not ready and willing
To make a big decision like this
And it could ruin the rest of our lives
You said

All he did was cause you harm
Me I'll be your good luck charm
So run to my arms
If you want someone to keep you nice and warm

By:James Watson

Jobs

Like a therapist
Let me relieve you from some stress
We going to need a housekeeper
To clean up this mess
Call me a chef
Because you taste so damn good
Like a carpenter
You can play with this wood
Like a bus driver
You can go for a ride
Call me your dentist
Open your mouth up real wide
While I come inside
I'll be your beautician
Let me grab you by the hair
Like a HVAC technician
You'll be begging me for air
If you going to do the job
Do it right
Because I can work all day and all night

By:James Watson

Just a little bit

Can I spend the night
For just a little bit
Can I hold you tight
For just a little bit
Can I relax your mind
For just a little bit
Can we bump and grind
For just a little bit
Can I play with it
For just a little bit
Can I stay in it
For just a little bit
Can I beat it up
For just a little bit
Can I eat it up
For just a little bit
Can I tease you
For just a little bit
Can I please you
For just a little bit

By:James Watson

Kamala Harris

Kamala Harris
You gave every women a chance
To strive harder under no circumstance
To push yourself far
And go beyond the north star
You put aside
All of your pride
And opened our eyes up very wide
To possibilities
That every girl
In this dominate man's world
Can be treated the same
Not only are you the picture
That says a thousand words
But you're also the frame
That keeps everything together
And have this picture looking more beautiful than ever
Thank you for your strength
That we may further our length
Thank you for your wisdom
And your mind
That we may see pass all the criticism
That has kept our women blind

Because now we can see
That we have the same abilities
As any man
It's all apart of God's plan
That you may be seated at his right hand
As he guides you and take
you to the Promised Land

By:James Watson

Katrina

The year was 2005
Hurricane Katrina made land fall
She took many lives
A few would survive
New Orleans felt her wrath
As she destroyed everything in her path
Bodies washed away to the shores
As the waters were filled with blood and gore
New Orleans never seen anything like this before
They warn people to evacuate
But it was too late
Some never wanted to leave their home
As they packed everyone at the Super Dome
Red cross tried to help
But it was just too much to bare
Then Kanye West got on the air
And said that George Bush doesn't care
About black people
He said that people are dying down here
And what you see on television can't compare
To what you'll see once you're down there
This is our home
And we're not going anywhere

By: James Watson

Knives

It's like a thousand knives
Stabbing me in the heart
You're known for taking lives
And tearing people apart
You cut me so deep
It hurts so bad
At night I can't even get any sleep
I'm scared for life
Whoever thought you would take this knife
And stick it in my back
As soon as I turned away
That's when you decided to attack
Now all I can do is shout
Please take it out!!!!!
Trying to catch my breath
I thought that you would care
But you just watch me bleed to death

By:James Watson

Last Days

We're living in the last days
There's so much evil across the world
The bible is showing itself in so many ways
Jesus is coming back for us
Will you be ready
The bible will fulfill its promise
When the seven trumpets blow
The world will then know
That the end is near
So do not fear
Bodys will be raised
The Lord we shall praise
Until all knees have bowed down
And all heads have looked up to the crown
There will be wrath
And a bloodbath
We must go through this
Before we can reach the other side
The groom is coming back to get his bride

By:James Watson

Lead Me

Lord lead me down the path
you want me to follow
Don't lead me down a path that's hollow
Lord lead me to your grace
Lead me to your holy place
Lead me away from harm
Lord lead me not into a storm
But lead me right to your arms
Lord me away from darkness
And lead me right to your righteousness
Lead me not into temptation
But lead me right to your salvation
Lord lead me right to your heart
Lead me to a brand new start
Lord lead me away from man
And all his evil plans
Lead me right to the Promised Land
That I shall be able to stand
Next to your right hand

By:James Watson

Lebron James

My name
Is Lebron James
And if anyone tell you
They'll tell you that I got game
Slam dunking on these fools
I'm the leader of the new school
Dropping points
And breaking joints
No one can test my skills
Because I'm ill
Every time I score
I give them the chills
The crowd wants to see more
You can't win without me
I'm everything these players want to be
I'm the face of sports
Everyone knows when I hit the court
I'm going for it all
So pass me the ball
I will not stop
Until I'm on top
I'm everyone's idol
Put me on your team
If you want to win a NBA title

By:James Watson

Let your voice be heard

I pray for those who's going
through domestic violence
Let your voice be heard
Don't be left in silence
It's not your fault
What you're going through
It could of happen to any one of us
It just happened to happen to you
You're not the one to blame
So don't you dare feel ashamed
Verbal mental or physical
It's all the same
The weak
Will not speak
But the strong
Will not allow this to go on but so long
Putting your hands on someone is wrong
No matter how you look at it

By:James Watson

Life's a bitch

Is it me
Or do I have bad luck
Because life just don't give a fuck
About someone like me
I'm about to lose my mind
And it seems like I can't keep up
With the rest of society
I've falling so far behind
And it's driving me crazy
I don't know where to begin
Should I give up and throw the towel in
Nothing is going my way
And I don't know how I'm making it
From day to day
I don't know how I lasted this long
But it's by the grace of God
That's keeping me strong
That I'm able to hold on
Even when life gets a little hard
Because life's a bitch and then you die
But I will always keep my head to the sky

By:James Watson

Light a candle

I'm about to light a candle
And it will be so relaxing
Tonight I'm about to give you more than you can handle
While I'm giving you a good waxing
I'm about to burn
One for tonight
As I turn
Off the light
I can smell your fragrance
And it's putting me in a trance
With one flick of this match
Watch me make the perfect catch
You got that fire
That has me burning with desire

By:James Watson

Like Mike dedicated to Michael Jordan

Everyone wants to be like Mike
He took the game of basketball to newer heights
He played basketball and baseball
He could do it all
He won 6 titles in his career
Look at him go
As he flies through the air
Everyone knew his name in the street
From Gatorade
To Hanes
And air jordans on his feet
This brother was unique
And everyone love his technique
The best player alive
From number 23
To the number 45
He strive
To become the best
And he didn't rest
Until he conquered his quest
Six foot six and slim
One thing he knew how to do

Was put that ball in the rim
He's the player other players feared the most
So beware when you see him coming through the post
He's the greatest of all time
No one could stop him
When he was in his prime

By:James Watson

Lost

I thought my life was through
When I lost you
I keep thinking about you
Thought I couldn't go on without you
It hurts me to my heart
To see us seperated apart
I lose sleep at night
And holding back these tears
Is too much for me to fight
Losing you was one of my biggest fears
I want to break everything in sight
Because I know getting over you
is going to take some years
My heart is crushed
And my feelings been flushed
Down the drain
Because all I feel is pain
I know one day I will get over this
But until then
You'll be truly missed

By:James Watson

Lottery Ticket

They say
I have beginners luck
Because she makes me feel like a million bucks
They told me not to gamble with my life
But I hit the jackpot
When she became my wife
She's my mega million
She's my Powerball
And I'm playing to win it all
They say
That gambling is a sin
But the more I play
The better the chances I have to win
So I'm going to try my luck anyway
I have the winning ticket
Right here in my hand
And I'm the luckiest man
On this planet

By:James Watson

Love and Hip Hop

Love and Hip Hop
Needs to stop
People selling themselves just to get to the top
This show is nothing but drama
And people sleeping around with other people baby fathers and baby mama
This show is having a real impact
On our kids lives
They want you to believe
This is how we act
This show is messing with our kids mind
People acting like animals
Showing off their behind
This show isn't real
Most of them are fake
Women sleeping around with everyone
Just for a record deal
Men acting like male whores
Sleeping around with every other woman
But we all know what goes on behind closed doors
They be acting real tough
When the camera is on

But when the camera goes off
They be acting real soft
This show is a disgrace
And give a bad example for the black race

By:James Watson

Love in the club

I've made love in the tub
And in the back seat of a car
But I've never made love in the club
This is the best by far
We dancing
And romancing
You said you don't care who look
And to not judge a book
By its cover
Because by the end of the song
I'll be your secret lover
What we're doing is wrong
But you don't care
You can do this all night long
I told her
You're not messing with a scrub
I'm the type of guy
Who would shoot up your club

By:James Watson

Love in the studio

We making love in the booth
No one can hear us
Because it's soundproof
Ecstacy is what I'm bringing
I love how you grab my mic
And started singing
I'm about to lay down a track
While I'm arching your back
I'm pushing all of your buttons
Then you started to take your clothes off
All of a sudden
I want to see you hit that high note
As we make love to the song I wrote
Can you give me sixteen bars
While I'm playing with your guitar
By the end of the night
You will be a star

By:James Watson

Loyal to the wrong one

People are loyal to the one
Who treat them wrong
And not loyal to the one
Who had your back for so long
These are the one you're loyal to
The one who don't give a fuck about you
Where are they at
When you need someone to have your back
They're nowhere to be found
But these are the one you keep around
The one that shows you respect
You neglect
And the one that neglect you
You show respect to
I just don't understand
How you can call these type of people
Your right hand man

By: James Watson

Make it or Take it

I'm going to make it
Even if that means
I have to take it
It's my way
Or the highway
I'm knocking down all of my competition
And I'm doing it with intervention
I will never back down from a fight
I'm destroying everything in sight
I'm a triple threat
And I can't let them see me sweat
See I'm not fine
Until I reach the finish line
And once I do
Then it would definitely be mine
See I was manifest
To become my best
And I will not rest
Until I've conquered my quest

By:James Watson

Michael Jackson

There would be no Jackson five
Without Michael Jackson
He was the greatest artist alive
Michael Jackson had hits
Like smooth criminal, billy jean and beat it
Michael Jackson couldn't only sing
He could also dance
Michael Jackson gave us the most greatest performance
Michael Jackson will forever be in our hearts
He had the most number one hits
On the billboard top 100 charts
Michael Jackson made a killer
With his album thriller
The world fell in love
With his glitter sock and glove
He was a mastermind
And truly one of a kind
Michael Jackson love the kids
And it's sad what happened to him
The way it did

By:James Watson

Miracle Whip

Girl what's a sandwich without miracle whip
It's nothing
So let me spread it across your lip
It's creamy and white
And taste good with every bite
It's not heavy at all
It's very lite
And could cure any appetite
They say it goes better with bread
But I rather put it on you instead
Once you had this mayo
You can't say no
That's how good it taste
You just can't let it go to waste

By:James Watson

Mistakes

I made some mistakes in my past
I had to slow down
Because I was moving too fast
If I knew what I knew now
Maybe what I had would have last
Now I'm sitting around
Looking for you
But you're nowhere to be found
I regret the day
I treated you so bad
I regret the day
I made you so mad
Hurting you was my only concern
But you know what they say
You live and you learn
Because now you're gone away
And I'm wishing somehow you would return
Back to me someday
Because now I have to let it burn
And this is the price I have to pay

By:James Watson

Monster

I'm the monster that you created in me
I'm the monster no one wanted to see
I'm this way because of you
I'm this way because of what you put me through
I'm the monster inside of your head
I'm the monster underneath your bed
I'm the monster that lurks in the night
I'm the monster that brings you fright
I'm the monster that's hard to kill
I'm the monster that love to see your blood spill
I'm the monster that gives you the chills
I'm the monster that brings you thrill
I'm the monster that will not go away
I'm the monster that will make you pay

By:James Watson

Mr. Officer

It's us versus the police
And we're not trying to fight
We just want peace
And equal rights
You're supposed to protect and serve
A lot of things you've done to us
We didn't deserve
We keep taking the same abuse
And you keep using the same excuse
We're not criminals
So stop treating us like we're animals
We will not resist
But you still want to throw the handcuffs
On our wrist
So we pump our fist
Because we refuse to be another black man
On your target list

By:James Watson

My apology letter

Forgive me
I never meant to hurt you
I promise if you forgive me
I'll never do it again boo
How could I do such a thing
How could I clip your pretty wings
I know the hurt in your heart
Hurts worse than a bee sting
Like a puppet I pulled you by the string
If you leave me today
I'll understand
Because I haven't been a good man
I lied to your face
Then have the nerve to show up at your place
You said you can't do this anymore
That you need some space
It's going to hurt my pride
Knowing you're not by my side
But I've done it to myself
And it's going to hurt me to
see you with someone else
Can't complain now
Just have to do better
So I hope you except my apology letter

By:James Watson

Never Doubt Her

Never doubt her
Because you know you can't do it without her
Always let her know that you're thinking about her
Be smart
And never break her heart
Because that's when she'll depart
Go the extra mile
To make her smile
Show her something you never did for her in a while
Never run or hide
From her feelings that she has inside
Show her that you'll always be there to provide
Never make her cry
Never tell her a lie
Always be willing to give it another try
Don't play games
Or call her out her name
Because she'll never look at you the same
Don't be afraid to show how much you care
Don't be afraid to show how much you're willing to spare
Don't be afraid to show how much you're willing to share

Because every women needs that support
And every women needs that man comfort
Because love isn't a game
So don't treat it like a sport

By:James Watson

Never ever

Never ever
Have I seen someone as beautiful as you
Never ever
Have I seen someone who can
do the things you can do
Never ever
Have I seen someone with such a beautiful smile
Never ever
Have I seen someone with so much style
Never ever
Have I seen someone who's so smart
Never ever
Have I seen someone with such a beautiful heart
Never ever
Have I seen someone with so much integrity
Never ever
Have I seen someone with so much dignity
Never ever
Have I seen someone who's so classy
Never ever
Have I seen someone who can be so sassy

By:James Watson

No good in goodbye

There's no good in goodbye
The reason why it never worked out
Was because
We never saw eye to eye
Maybe if we had more understanding
Instead of you always being so demanding
Things might have been more different
But you've played with my intelligence
Thought I had no common sense
How long was you going to play this game
Before you got caught
The reason why things
haven't been the same
Was because
You never been taught
How to love someone's heart
All you've been used to
was breaking them apart
You've never seen the real art
Of someone's feeling
Because all you've been dealing
with was broken hearts
And that's the reason why
It never felt appealing

By:James Watson

No matter what you're going through

No matter what you're going through
Always put me first
No matter what you're going through
Remember there's always someone going through something much worst
No matter what you're going through
I will always be by your side
No matter what you're going through
I will always provide
No matter what you're going through
Never forget about me
No matter what you're going through
Never doubt me
No matter what you're going through
Do not fear
No matter what you're going through
My love is near
No matter what you're going through
I will be there to wipe your tears away
No matter what you're going through
Get on your knees and pray
No matter what you're going through

Look to the cross
No matter what you're going through
Remember my loss

By:James Watson

Not letting nothing get in my way

I got to do
What I got to do
I'm not letting nothing get in my way
Not even you
Because at the end of the day
It's all about me
And no matter what you say
I'm going to be
Who I'm going to be
I gave you too much satisfaction
And you will no longer be a distraction
I will succeed
Even when you think I'm not
And in case you forgot
Let me remind you again
With or without you
I will win

By:James Watson

Nothing to Something

People put me down
Told me I wouldn't be nothing
But look at me now
I rise above everything
They told me I wouldn't last very long
Boy were they wrong
In the midst of everything
God kept me strong
I stop listening to them
And start listening to him
Because at the end of the day
It only matters what he has to say
All they wanted to do was hold me back
But I refuse to let them take me off track
See they just trying to take me off focus
But like magic
I made them disappear like hocus pocus
Now I just smile in the haters face
Because they wish they were in my place
I'm not mad at them
Because their words I embrace
And it wasn't them

Why I made it this far
But because of God's grace
That made me a star

By:James Watson

Oreo

I can't get enough
Of your double stuff
I want to dunk my oreo cookie
In a tall glass of milk
Swallow your nookie
As it goes down my throat smooth like silk
I'm a pro at it
I'm far from a rookie
I want to lick the middle
While I play with your cat
Like a fiddle
It's every man fantasy and dream
To have a threesome
With a black and white girl
I call them cookies and cream
I like it thin or thick
But no matter which one I pick
I'm giving it a lick

By:James Watson

Paul Mooney

When every wolfe howls at the full moon
And every bird sing at high noon
Paul Mooney was more loony
Then any loony tune
He wrote for the greatest comic
Like Richard Pryor and Redd Foxx
Paul Mooney wasn't like any other comic
He thought outside the box
His jokes made you feel uncomfortable
And sometimes can be controversial
He made you laugh
When he told a joke
You'll be laughing so hard
Until you start to choke
He gave it to you raw
And didn't give a damn about the law
He spoke his mind
And his jokes were one of a kind
He didn't discriminate
Who he made fun of
Because at the end of the day
It was all about love

By:James Watson

Pinocchio

You keep telling these lies
Your nose will start to grow
Pinocchio
How can you look at me with a straight face
And tell me a bold face lie
You have no shame in what you do
And that's a disgrace
Then you got the nerve to look me in the eyes
Like I wasn't going to see right through you
A lie can destroy a person's pride
And can destroy everything you're feeling inside
The truth will set you free
A lie will keep you held down in captivity
A lie will deceive you
And make it hard for someone to believe you

By:James Watson

Piece of trash

You must like being treated like a piece of trash
You let every man in the neighborhood smash
And all they had to do was show you some cash
How could you disrespect yourself like that
And how could you neglect yourself like that
You have no shame in what you do
And you can't blame no one for
what you've been through
You have to know your worth
And put yourself first
You're a blessing to this earth
But you feel like you're a curse
Don't give it up so easily
Don't be so sleazy
You're God's greatest creation
You don't always have to show your body off
Leave something to the imagination
Make him work for it
Because your body is sacred

By:James Watson

Please don't shoot

My hands are up
Please don't shoot
But you're going to do it anyway
So since you've done that
We're going to loot
And we don't give a damn what you have to say
We're tired of being treated this way
You said that your life was on the line
That's the same excuse you use all the time
You think what you're doing is fine
I committed no crime
So let me go officer please
But before I could say anything
You told me to get on my knees
As you aimed your gun at my head
You said if I made one false move
That I was dead

By:James Watson

Popping Pills

I can't stop popping these pills
Now I'm starting to have the chills
I'm sweating
And the side effects can be life threatening
I can feel the rush of adrenaline
Going through my veins
I'm addicted to ecstacy, penicillin
Opioids
Percocets
And steroids
My family wants me to stop using these pills
They say I'm abusing these pills
Even though they make me a little high
I need them to get by
They say I look like a crackhead
When I take them
And they say if I don't stop taking them
That one day I might overdose
And end up somewhere dead
I don't expect them to understand
I just need them to give me a helping hand

By:James Watson

Precious Baby Girl

Welcome to the world
My precious baby girl
I promise to always be by your side
You will make someone a beautiful bride
Anything you need from me
I promise to provide
To hold you in my arms
Is such a charm
You keep my heart nice and warm
I will keep you away from harm
I can't stop every man from breaking your heart
But if he puts his hands on you
I will rip him apart
You can always come to me when you need to talk
Never argue with a man
Just take a deep breath
And go for a walk
I can't wait until that day
When I walk you down that aisle
And give you away
I hope you find someone like me
Who would love you
The way I do

By:James Watson

Rise

Rise to the ocassion
Rise in any situation
Rise to the top
Rise and never stop
Rise above the ground
Rise and never let them see you down
Rise and make a stand
Rise and let your wings expand
Rise and pump your fist
Rise because we will get hrough this
Rise for what's right
Rise even though you don't have the stregth to fight

By:James Watson

September 11 2021

20 years later
We still mourn
And the devastation still leaves us torn
The pain
Still remain
Who should pay the cost
For thousands of Americans lives being lost
The hate still builds in our heart
But we should not let that tear us apart
Because we're stronger than that
And we will bounce back
We will never forget the attack
On the twin towers
As we lay flowers
For those who lost their lives
You may have taken our pride
But you will never take the spirit we have inside
We're the greatest country in the land
Divided we fall
United we stand

By: James Watson

Shaquille O'Neal

They call him
Shaquille O'Neal
Also known as
The man of steel
It's Shaq attack
And he's breaking back
As he slam dunk
On these punks
Dominating the paint
If you think you can stop him
You can't
Because he's tearing down the rim
You better watch out
Because when he has the ball
He's coming at you with full force
You would have thought you've ran into a brick wall
He played with some of the best
So when you see that S on his chest
You better make way
Because he came to play

By:James Watson

Single Mothers

Your baby daddy is never home
Raising three kids on your own
Single mother on welfare
Struggling trying to feed your kids
And find them a proper daycare
You need a little support
But the only way you will get that
Is if you take him down to court
You're losing your mind
Trying to go to school and
work at the same time
I salute you
For doing all of this
And still staying on your grind
You're fighting so hard to not
let this keep you down
You smile to hide your frown
You're at social service everyday
So they will not take your benefits away
That's your only way of
putting food on the table
You may not have it all
At least you're stable

All you're asking for is that he call
Or come by on the kids birthday or holiday
It hurts that it has to be this way
But what else can you do
If he's not going to be there for the kids and you

By:James Watson

Sleeping with the enemy

It's like I'm sleping with the enemy
Because lately
It seems like you're no longer in to me
Do you hate me
This bed is so cold
And at night
I just need someone warm to hold
Did I get you mad
And if I done something
wrong I apologize
I think it's sad
That we can't look each other in the eyes
When we're sleeping
Are you creeping
What are you keeping
From me
Because lately
You've been acting kind of strange
And something about you
is starting to change

By:James Watson

Sleepless in Seattle

Last night I cried myself to sleep
The cut you put on my heart was deep
My pillow is so soak and wet
I'll be damn if I let
Someone like you break my heart
I'll be damn if I let
Someone like you tear me apart
Another sleepless night in Seattle
When you made me cry
You already loss this battle
I'm tired of going on this emotional
roller coaster ride with you
I'm tired of holding all of my feelings inside for you
I hate going to bed mad
That's why we should make up now
I know this night started off bad
For both of us
But it doesn't have to end this way
Whatever happened tonight
Doesn't have to carry on to the next day

By:James Watson

So many

So many had doubts
So many counted me out
So many said I would fail
So many said I wouldn't prevail
So many said I wouldn't achieve
So many didn't believe
So many said I wasn't worth it
So many said I wouldn't be shit
So many said I don't have what it takes
So many said I would fail
because of my mistakes
But I prove all of them wrong
Because when they thought I gave up
I kept coming back strong

By:James Watson

Sometimes

Sometimes it's okay to cry
Sometimes it's okay to give it another try
Sometimes it's okay to frown
Sometimes it's okay to be a little down
Sometimes it's okay not to look someone in the eye
Sometimes it's okay to say goodbye
Sometimes it's okay to be wrong
Sometimes it's okay to play along
Sometimes it's okay to lose
Sometimes it's okay to chose
Sometimes it's okay to show a little fear
Sometimes it's okay to lend a ear
Sometimes it's okay to feel these things
Because you never know the joy it will bring

By:James Watson

Taking credit for everything we do

White man always taking credit
For everything that we do
But don't want to give credit
For what we been through
They want to be us so bad
But when we try to be them
They get mad
They want to walk like us
And talk like us
Until you become a slave
You can never be us
`Until you've been beating and misbehave
You can never be us
My people went through hell
To get where we are today
Just for a white man
To take it all away

By:James Watson

Tell him

Tell him
That you and him will never be
Tell him
That he would never compare to me
Tell him
To stop telling you these lies
Tell him
To be a man and look you in your eyes
Tell him
That you're not going to have it anymore
Tell him
To leave your keys at the front door
Tell him
That it's over and that you've found another man
Tell him
That he would never love you like I can
Tell him
That you need some space
Tell him
That someone else is taking his place
Tell him
That you're moving on
Tell him

That he's going to miss you while you're gone

Tell him

That you've found someone
that would love you for you

Tell him

Before I do

By:James Watson

That's my son

That's my son
Who you're trying to attack
That's my son
Who knees you have on his back
That's my son
You're holding down
That's my son
You have on the ground
That's my son
Who you're trying to arrest
That's my son
Who you shot in the chest
That's my son
Who you've killed
That's my son
Who blood you've spilled

By: James Watson

The God I serve

You gave me things I didn't even deserve
Everyday you remind me of the God I serve
Bless are those who worship your name
Curse are those who come to
you for richest and fame
When I couldn't go another length
You carried me along
When I had no strength
You kept me strong
I thank you from the bottom of my heart
The devil is jealous of our relationship
And that's why he wants to tear us apart
But he will not succeed
Because your love for me is guaranteed
This is one battle he doesn't want to fight
His darkness will never overcome your light
My life doesn't belong to him
It belongs to you
So I will not listen or do
What he ask me to
See he wants me to fail
Lock me down
And throw me in jail

But he will not prevail
As long as you're around
He can't take me down

By:James Watson

The hill we climb dedicated to Amanda Gorman

The hill we climb is steep
And when we come down that hill it's deep
We never know what we'll see
Once when get to the top
Just know that when we come down it
It's a long drop
We all want to climb that hill one day
But there's so many things
that will get in our way
Is there something waiting for us
On the other side
Should we walk
Until our feet hurt
Or should we go for a ride
Over the gravel and dirt
We will not stop
Until we've made it to the top
We will not stop
Until we're the king of the crop
Once we've made it over the hill
Then we can rest
And once we've made it over the hill
Then we've conquered our quest

By:James Watson

The Ladawn Black Show

Welcome to the Ladawn Black show
I got the right songs
That will make your body flow
I'm on the air all night long
So call in
While I let this record spin
I got some r&b classics
Sure to make your body move
And put you in the grove
Tonight I'm playing nothing but the best
So call in with your request
And let Ladawn Black put you to rest
Nobody can play the hits like I do
Tonight I want to hear from you
We will be jamming
And slamming
All your favorite tracks
So sit back
And enjoy the show
With your host Ladawn Black

By:James Watson

The only woman

How could I let you the only woman
I could call my wife
Walk out of my life
My selfishness
And foolishness
Caused you a lot of pain
I lied to you
When I told you that I wouldn't do it again
No one deserves what I put you through
I can say I'm sorry a thousand times
It's still not going to change your mind
The damage is already done
I'm sorry that you had to be the one
It's not fair
And it's too late
To try and show you that I care
So I understand
If you want to be with another man
Why would you want to stay
With someone who doesn't
give you the time or the day

You would be a fool to let someone like me

Treat you this way

You shouldn't have to pay

For my mistakes

By:James Watson

The Plandemic

Was this pandemic planned
Was this pandemic created by man
Then you called this a Chinese disease
So you just going to tell us anything
And expect us to believe it
Please!!!!
It's funny how this virus
Came out the same time as the census
Pay attention y'all
They trying to get rid of us
Then to cover everything up
They want to give us a stimulus check
Now we're in a economic struggle
Man this country is a wreck
Now we have to walk around
with masks on our face
Like we're wearing a muzzle
Now people walking around paranoid
Trying their best to avoid
Catching this thing called Covid 19
And they said it would be a year
Before they find a vaccine
Now the whole world walking around in fear

By:James Watson

This isn't right

Slowly open your door
And move away from the car
Officer may I ask what I'm being stop for
Put your hands in the air
Where I can see them
Okay Officer what seems to be the problem
Where were you at such and such time
Look Officer I committed no crime
This isn't right
Why do you have these cuffs on me so tight
I don't want to lose my life
I'm just trying to make it home
To my kids and my wife
Why you so nervous
You know why
This is how I act
Anytime I see a cop drive by
I see to many cops stopping young men like me
For no reason at all
Harass and thrown up against the wall
You may go
We've found nothing on you
Have a nice day
Whatever Officer you too

By:James Watson

Trials and Tribulations

The best way to deal with
your trials and tribulations
Is to first identify the situation
Things in life will hold you back
But if you pray to God
He'll put your life back on track
We all have ups and downs
And the best thing to do in
this situation is to smile
And not frown
Because God can turn any situation around
When you feel like you've been
beaten down to the ground
Never give up
And never give in
Because when situations erupt
God will make sure that you win

By:James Watson

Trust in God

Trust in God

And everything else will fall in place

Trust in God

And he will show you his mercy and grace

Trust in God

And he will always have your back

Trust in God

And he will protect you from the devil when he's trying to attack

Trust in God

And he will never leave your side

Trust in God

And he will always be there to provide

Trust in God

Because he's your only friend

Trust in God

Because he will be there for you until the very end

By:James Watson

Unbelievable

Girl you're so unbelievable
And you're so over achievable
Your love is so underrated
And your love is so appreciated
They say that love is blind
And true love is so hard to find
But I say it's all in your mind
Because the love you give is so gentle and kind
I must be dreaming
Because this seems so unreal
It's so unbelievable
How much your heart has to reveal
It's so unbelievable
How much your love can heal
I've never seen anyone like you before
And this is the main reason
why I want you even more
Because you're so unbelievable

By:James Watson

Veteran Day

We salute you
Our country appreciates all the
hard battles you've been through
To keep us the greatest country in the land
If it wasn't for you making a stand
For what you believe in
We probably would have fell in the hands
Of our enemies
You serve a lot
And deserve a lot
Thank you for putting your life on the line
Just to make sure the citizens of this country are fine
Thank you for paying the price
And making the ultimate sacrifice
Just to make sure that we're free
Thank you for serving your country

By:James Watson

We shall overcome

Our nation will rise
Our nation will fall
We will not be defeated
But we shall rise through it all
And if we fail
Then we will prevail
We shall overcome
All the accusation
All the allegation
They say about our country
For nothing shall hold us down
Because our foot is on solid ground
For we are the greatest country in this land
Divided we fall
United we shall stand
We will never give up
But we shall fight
By the dawn early light
In God we trust
We will rise above the ashes and dust
If we believe everything they
say about our country
That wasn't true
Then we wouldn't be

The red
The white
And the blue

By:James Watson

Wendy Williams

Wendy Williams you're
nothing but a gossip queen
Always talking about things
you've never been through
Or never seen
All you do is attack
People who can't fight back
Stop putting your nose where it doesn't belong
Because what you're doing is wrong
You're only doing this for fame
Which is so damn lame
You think you're better than us
When you're just the same
The industry got you tame
You're only doing this so people
can remember your name
You only do what they tell you to do
And that's a damn shame
You need to be slapped in your face
Your show is a disgrace
And someone needs to put you in your place
You're a tran
And you look like a man
You need to take that wig off
And throw it in the trash can

Looking like someone smacked
you in the face with a frying pan
I don't know where you get your news
But you're only doing this to get views
Because half of the things you say
Is bullshit anyway

By:James Watson

What's Love

What's love
Does it comes from above
Are we a perfect pair
Like hand and glove
What's love
When all we do is push and shove
If we're in love
Does that mean that we're one
If we hate one another
Does that mean that we're done
What's love
And why does it play so many games
What's love
And why does it makes me want
to give you my last name
What's love
And why is it so blind
What's love
And why is it so hard to find
What's love
And why does it hurts so bad
What's love
Could this be the best feeling that we ever had

By:James Watson

When we touch

When we touch
I start to melt
When we touch
It's the best feeling that I've ever felt
When we touch
I can feel the sensation
When we touch
I can feel the infatuation
When we touch
It's simply amazing
When we touch
I need you like a bad craving
When we touch
I become hot
When we touch
You know where to hit my spot
When we touch
It just feels so right
When we touch
I want to make love to you all day and all night

By:James Watson

Withdraw

I can't get no sleep at night
Because I'm tossing and turning in my bed
Something doesn't seem right
Because I can't get you out of my head
You got me sweating and some more
I never felt this way before
My heart is starting to race
And I can't stand in one place
My feet are starting to pace
Back and forth
What happening to me
Because I got it bad
This is the worst feeling I've ever had
Itching and twitching
I can't stay still
Should I just chill
And take a pill
How would this make me feel
Or am I really ill

By:James Watson

Woman

Every man needs a woman
To be his backbone
God created a woman
Because he knew man couldn't do it alone
Woman are strong when it comes to the heart
And when it comes to the mind
Woman are very smart
Man may plant the seed
But woman nourish the soul
When they breastfeed
Man are the barrier
When it comes to his wife
But woman are the carrier
When it comes to life
Don't argue with a woman
When it comes to a fight
Because even if a man hates to admit it
A woman is always right

By:James Watson

You can still

You can still be funny without cursing

You can still have a
conversation without fussing

You can still be sad without crying

You can still be bad without trying

You can still be sweet
without being charming

You can still be street without harming

You can still be pretty
without having an attitude

You can still make love
without being nude

You can still be nice and
still have your heart broken

You can still be quiet
and still be outspoken

You can still see and still be blind

You can still be free and still
not have a piece of mind

You can still be smart and still be dumb

You can still have feelings
and still be numb

By:James Watson

You smell

You smell too bad
To want to be all up in someone's face
You smell so bad
It's starting to smell up the whole place
Step back and give me some space
Did you take a bath today
Why do you smell this way
I can't stand the funk
You smell like a skunk
You smell like feces and piss
You're to grown to be smelling like this
I'm not trying to be rude
But you stink
And you wonder why I have an attitude
You have a stench
And you need to drench
Yourself in some soap and water
You need to take a shower
Your smell is starting to over power
My nose
You smell like you're decompose
And that's sad
That you smell this bad

By:James Watson

You will not be satisfied

You will not be satisfied
Until I'm gone
You will not be satisfied
Until I've move on
You will not be satisfied
Until I've made you cry
You will not be satisfied
Until I've left you hanging out to dry
You will not be satisfied
Until I've walk out that door
You will not be satisfied
Until I've told you I can't take it anymore
You will not be satisfied
Until I've found someone else
You will not be satisfied
Until I've left you all by yourself
You will not be satisfied
Until the same thing happened to you
You will not be satisfied
Until you've felt what I've been through

By:James Watson

Your eyes

When I look into your eyes
I'm mesmerized
When I look into your eyes
I become hypnotized
When I look into your eyes
I become paralyzed
When I look into your eyes
It's like watching the sun rise
When I look into your eyes
It takes me by surprise
When I look into your eyes
I can see where heaven lies
Because this is what I see
When I look into your eyes

By:James Watson

Zaytoven

Zaytoven the founder of trap music
He brung a different style to rap music
Zaytoven got the beats
If you need that heat
A legend in these streets
A role model to so many producers out here
His music is unlike anything
you have ever heard out there
Him and Gucci Mane created
a new era in hip hop
Zaytoven had a dream of
going straight to the top
And once he got there
That he was never going to stop
Until his album dropped
He gave hip hop a new sound
You know when Zaytoven comes around
He's bringing nothing but fire
Zaytoven has inspired
A lot of artists out there
To push themselves higher
To continue to make dope tracks
And to never look back

By:James Watson

Author Biography

Welcome to my seventh book titled Deeper in life.In this book I go deeper into life.A lot has happen in the world that we live in.The pandemic has change all of our lives.What use to be normal is no longer.Today people are spending more time in their homes.And are looking for ways to find time for the things they love the most.And this is where books are now more important then ever.I tell stories and events that have shaken our lives.Deeper in life goes deeper into todays problems.And hopefully when you read this book it will solve all your issues that you may have or looking for.

My name is James Watson.The oldest of my siblings.I am a role model to my brothers and sisters.I am a Baltimore native.Born and raised here all of my life.One day I hope to travel the world.I have a passion for writing and telling stories.I hope one day my talent will take me far.Before I leave this earth I want to lay my mark on peoples lives.I want to be remembered as a great writer.

www.ingramcontent.com/pod-product-compliance
Lightning Source LLC
LaVergne TN
LVHW040146080526
838202LV00042B/3048